Dear Parents:

Congratulations! Your child is taking the first steps on an exciting journey. The destination? Independent reading!

STEP INTO READING® will help your child get there. The program offers five steps to reading success. Each step includes fun stories and colorful art or photographs. In addition to original fiction and books with favorite characters, there are Step into Reading Non-Fiction Readers, Phonics Readers and Boxed Sets, Sticker Readers, and Comic Readers—a complete literacy program with something to interest every child.

Learning to Read, Step by Step!

Ready to Read Preschool–Kindergarten
• big type and easy words • rhyme and rhythm • picture clues
For children who know the alphabet and are eager to begin reading.

Reading with Help Preschool–Grade 1
• basic vocabulary • short sentences • simple stories
For children who recognize familiar words and sound out new words with help.

Reading on Your Own Grades 1–3
• engaging characters • easy-to-follow plots • popular topics
For children who are ready to read on their own.

Reading Paragraphs Grades 2–3
• challenging vocabulary • short paragraphs • exciting stories
For newly independent readers who read simple sentences with confidence.

Ready for Chapters Grades 2–4
• chapters • longer paragraphs • full-color art
For children who want to take the plunge into chapter books but still like colorful pictures.

STEP INTO READING® is designed to give every child a successful reading experience. The grade levels are only guides; children will progress through the steps at their own speed, developing confidence in their reading.

Remember, a lifetime love of reading starts with a single step!

For Meghan, Caitlin, Nicole,
Joanna, and MegO —C.C.

To Silvina —D.B.

 Published in the United States by Random House Children's Books, a division of Penguin Random House LLC, 1745 Broadway, New York, NY 10019, and in Canada by Penguin Random House Canada Limited, Toronto. Random House and the colophon are registered trademarks of Penguin Random House LLC.

randomhousekids.com
dcsuperherogirls.com
dckids.com

ISBN 978-1-5247-6611-5 (trade) — ISBN 978-1-5247-6612-2 (lib. bdg.) —
ISBN 978-1-5247-6613-9 (ebook)

Printed in the United States of America

10 9 8 7 6 5 4 3 2 1

STEP INTO READING®

WELCOME TO SUPER HERO HIGH!

by Courtney Carbone

illustrated by Dario Briz

Random House New

Welcome to Super Hero High School!

Gifted students from all over the galaxy train here to become super heroes.

Wonder Woman, Supergirl, and Batgirl are students at Super Hero High School. They each have special powers and skills.

Wonder Woman is a born leader.
She is smart, strong, and brave.
With her Lasso of Truth,
she is ready for anything!

Supergirl is a powerful hero
with amazing strength and speed.
She also has X-ray and heat vision.

Batgirl is a skilled acrobat
and tech wizard who knows
how to save the day.
She uses Batarangs, Bat-Cuffs,
and other crime-fighting gear.

When bad guys show up,
the students spring into action!
The Save the Day Alarm
rings to alert everyone
when there is trouble.

Bad guys are no match
for these young heroes.

Wonder Woman, Supergirl, and

Batgirl have lots of classmates.

Harley Quinn, Katana, Bumblebee,
and Poison Ivy are just a few of them.

Students take ordinary classes
like history, art,
and science.

But often, amazing things happen!

Science experiments go wild, super-villains attack, and alien visitors arrive unexpectedly.

Students study hard to
become better super heroes.

In Flyers' Ed, they learn to dip, dodge, and dive through the obstacle course.

Flyers don't have all the fun. Students also learn to operate different vehicles.

Harley drives a bouncy buggy.

Wonder Woman flies her Invisible Jet.

And Batgirl rides a motorcycle!

In Weaponomics,
students are taught to create
and control all kinds of weapons.

And in Physical Education,
they learn to fight
and defend themselves.

In Super Suit Design,
students create new outfits
for any occasion.

Katana designs with
a keen sense of style
and a sharp sword.

During breaks, students can refuel and relax in the cafeteria.

They eat, do homework,
and talk to their friends.

At Super Hero High School,
students live on campus.

Their rooms reflect their different styles and personalities.

Students can also join clubs,
like the Junior Detective Society.

These activities make them
better students *and* better heroes!

The biggest honor is being named
Hero of the Month.
The students all do their best
in the hopes of receiving this award.

The students at Super Hero High School always work together to save the day!